What If...

Story by Regina J. Williams ✳ **Illustrations by Doug Keith**

ILLUMINATION
Arts
PUBLISHING COMPANY, INC.

I know it's
time for bed, Mom,
but what if . . .

My teddy bear could fly,
so I could ride him
to the nearest rainbow
and then stay awhile
to play.

And what if . . .

Dogs really did grow on
dogwood trees,
and I could pick a puppy
from a branch
and name her
Millie.

And what if . . .

Butterflies could sing,
and one flew in my window
every night to sing me
a lullaby.

And what if . . .

I had my own
special garden where I planted
candy hearts, marshmallow eggs,
and chocolate Santas, all in a row.

And what if . . .

Clouds suddenly became the
creatures they look like
and put on a show in the sky
just for me and my friends.

And what if . . .

Flowers tasted like lollipops,
and they grew really big
all around my bed.

And what if . . .

People everywhere would dance
and sing and be happy.

And there was only sunshine and love,
so all the scary monsters
would go away forever.

And what if...

All the trees would suddenly shrink
until they were the size of flowers,
and I could pick a bouquet
just for you, Mom.

And what if . . .

A shooting star
would fly into my pocket
and bring magic to my heart
forever.

And what if ...

It snowed silver and gold snowflakes
that sparkled like diamonds
and tasted like
peppermint ice cream.

And what if . . .

I made a great big seahorse out of clay,
then it came alive
and splashed around with me
in the bathtub.

And what if . . .

I had a real kangaroo for a pet,
and I could sleep in her pouch,
and her name was
Cornflower.

And what if . . .

I could raise my arms to touch the sky
and make a special rain
that would clean
the whole world.

And, Mom, what if … what if …

I had wings
and could fly through the
clouds, and . . . and . . .

"And now my little angel,
what if... we turn off the light,
so you can turn on your dream light
and dream your sweet dreams
all night long."

ILLUMINATION
Arts
PUBLISHING COMPANY, INC.
P.O. Box 1865, Bellevue, WA 98009
Tel: 425-644-7185 ★ 888-210-8216 (orders only) ★ Fax: 425-644-9274
liteinfo@illumin.com ★ www.illumin.com

Library of Congress Cataloging-in-Publication Data
Williams, Regina, 1958-
    What if– / written by Regina J. Williams; illustrated by Doug Keith.
       p. cm.
    Summary: A child speculates about flying teddy bears, flowers that taste like candy,
gold snowflakes, and more.
    ISBN 0-935699-22-8
    [1. Bedtime–Fiction. 2. Imagination–Fiction. 3. Dreams–Fiction.] I. Keith, Doug, ill.
II. Title.

PZ7.W6678 Wh 2001
[E]–dc21   00-054065

Published in the United States of America
Printed by Tien Wah Press of Singapore
Book Designer: Molly Murrah, Murrah & Company, Kirkland, WA

Author, Regina Williams

What If… began as a game between Regina Williams and her daughter Kayla. "One of us would say 'What if … could happen?' Then the other one would try to create an even more imaginative idea. The energy would build," Regina says, "as we came up with so many wild and fun possibilities, many of which are included in my story."

Growing up on a farm in northeast Texas, much of Regina's childhood entertainment came from books. A Magna Cum Laude graduate from the University of Texas, she is a speech and language pathologist in public schools. Regina and her husband live in the small town of New Boston, Texas with their daughters, Kayla and Grace. They also share their home with Millie, a miniature dachshund who is pleased to be featured in the story. *What If…* is Regina's first book.

Artist, Doug Keith

Doug Keith was delighted to illustrate *What If…* because of its focus on imagination. "This book provides an excellent opportunity to let your imagination soar and spiral way out of control!"

Doug modeled the main character after his ten-year-old daughter, Corie Lyn, who wasn't exactly thrilled to be portrayed as a boy. Corie Lyn's favorite teddy bear, Abner, and the family cat Merlin, also had modeling duties. However, Corie made sure Abner was back in her room at the end of the day.

After remodeling his Seattle home to create a spacious studio, Doug now commutes to work in comfy slippers. Widely known for his alphabet posters, he is currently illustrating *The Whoosh of Gadoosh*, another imaginative story for Illumination Arts.

Doug received his professional training at the Newark School of Fine and Industrial Arts. A versatile artist, he has received numerous accolades, including an Emmy for television graphics. His playful illustrations in *What If…* are a combination of watercolor and colored pencil.

The Illumination Arts Collection Of Inspiring Children's Books

ALL I SEE IS PART OF ME
Winner – 1996 *Award of Excellence — Body Mind Spirit Magazine*
By Chara Curtis, illustrated by Cynthia Aldrich $15.95   0-935699-07-4
In this international bestseller, a child finds the light within his heart and his common link with all of life.

THE BONSAI BEAR
Finalist—2000 *Children's Picture Book of the Year* — Coalition of Visionary Retailers
By Bernard Libster, illustrated by Aries Cheung $15.95   0-935699-15-5
Issa uses bonsai methods to keep his pet bear small, but the playful cub dreams of following his true nature.

CASSANDRA'S ANGEL
By Gina Otto, illustrated by Trudy Joost $15.95   0-935699-20-1
Cassandra feels lonely and misunderstood until her special angel shows her the truth within.

CORNELIUS AND THE DOG STAR
Winner – 1996 *Award of Excellence — Body Mind Spirit Magazine*
By Diana Spyropulos, illustrated by Ray Williams $15.95   0-935699-08-2
Grouchy old Cornelius Basset Hound can't enter Dog Heaven until he learns about love, fun, and kindness.

THE DOLL LADY
By H. Elizabeth Collins-Varni, illustrated by Judy Kuuisto $15.95   0-935699-24-4
The doll lady teaches children to treat dolls kindly and with great love, for they are just like people.

DRAGON
Winner –2000 *Children's Picture Book of the Year* — Coalition of Visionary Retailers
Written and Illustrated by Jody Bergsma $15.95   0-935699-17-1
Born on the same day, a gentle prince and a ferocious, fire-breathing dragon share a prophetic destiny.

DREAMBIRDS
1998 *Visionary Award for Best Children's Book – Coalition of Visionary Retailers*
By David Ogden, illustrated by Jody Bergsma $16.95   0-935699-09-0
A Native American boy battles his own ego as he searches for the elusive dreambird and its powerful gift.

FUN IS A FEELING
By Chara M. Curtis, illustrated by Cynthia Aldrich $15.95   0-935699-13-9
Find your fun! "Fun isn't something or somewhere or who. It's a feeling of joy that lives inside of you."

HOW FAR TO HEAVEN
By Chara M. Curtis, illustrated by Alfred Currier $15.95   0-935699-06-6
Exploring the wonders of nature, Nanna and her granddaughter discover heaven all around them.

LITTLE SQUAREHEAD
By Peggy O'Neill, illustrated by Denise Freeman $15.95   0-935699-21-X
Little Rosa overcomes the stigma of her unusual appearance after discovering a diamond glowing in her heart.

THE LITTLE WIZARD
Written and illustrated by Jody Bergsma $15.95   0-935699-19-8
Young Kevin discovers a wizard's cloak while on a perilous mission to save his mother's life.

ONE SMILE
By Cynthia McKinley, illustrated by Monica King $15.95   0-935699-23-6
The innocent smile of a young girl has far-reaching effects as it touches the lives of many people.

THE RIGHT TOUCH
Winner – Benjamin Franklin Parenting Award, Selected as Outstanding by the Parents Council

By Sandy Kleven, LCSW, illustrated by Jody Bergsma $15.95   0-935699-10-4

This beautifully illustrated read-aloud story teaches children how to prevent sexual abuse.

SKY CASTLE
"Children's Choice for 1999" by Children's Book Council

By Sandra Hanken, illustrated by Jody Bergsma $15.95   0-935699-14-7

Alive with dolphins, parrots and fairies, this magical tale inspires us to believe in the power of our dreams.

TO SLEEP WITH THE ANGELS
Finalist—2000 *Children's Picture Book of the Year* — Coalition of Visionary Retailers

By H. Elizabeth Collins, illustrated by Judy Kuusisto $15.95   0-935699-16-3

Comforting her to sleep each night, a young girl's guardian angel fills her dreams with magical adventures.

WINGS OF CHANGE

By Franklin Hill, Ph.D., illustrated by Aries Cheung $15.95   0-935699-18-X

A contented little caterpillar resists his approaching transformation into a butterfly.

U.S. Orders: add $2.00 postage; each additional book add $1.00. No postage if ordering 5 or more books.
Washington residents please add appropriate sales tax.

ILLUMINATION
Arts

PUBLISHING COMPANY, INC.

P.O. Box 1865, Bellevue, WA 98009 ★ Tel: 425-644-7185 ★ Fax: 425-644-9274

liteinfo@illumin.com ★ www.illumin.com

Now turn on
your dream light . . .

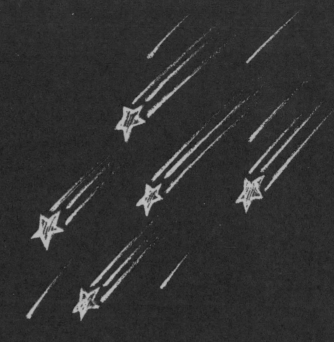